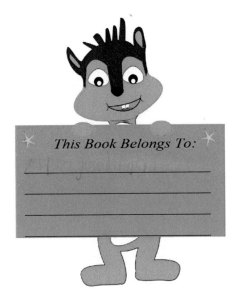

This Book Belongs To:

_____

_____

_____

For my little Darylings!
Jasmine, Alexis, Tatiana and Raquel

ISBN-13: 978-1514241769
ISBN-10: 1514241765

Cover design & images by Natasha Owens

Fluffy Tails

By Natasha Owens
Illustrated by Natasha Owens & Alexis Owens

Each morning after breakfast, Tatiana and Raquel open the back door to go outside and play in the yard.

Guess who comes running outside behind them one after the other or sometimes side by side?

Zeus and Xerxes

"Be careful!" Mom calls out.

"We will Mommy," Tatiana and Raquel shout as they head straight for the swings.

"Ruff! Ruff!" reply Zeus and Xerxes as they take off running towards the fence. On their way, Zeus and Xerxes run past the sandbox. As they do, Zeus shouts...

"STOP!"

The puppies quickly stop.

"What is it?" Xerxes asks.

"That!" Zeus exclaims and turns his head.

The brothers look in the sandbox and then at each other.

And they both shout...

"Someone has been in our backyard," Xerxes says.
"Do you know who those footprints belong to?"
they both ask.
"I don't know," Zeus says. "I don't know either,"
Xerxes says.

Let's find out. Let's ask...

Jon Dart!

Zeus and Xerxes immediately take off running across the yard and head for the swimming pool. When they reach the fence, they call out, "Jon Dart! Jon Dart! We found footprints!!!"

Jon Dart pokes his head out from his home under the diving board and says, "Hello Zeus! Hello Xerxes! Footprints?"

Jon Dart dips down into his hole and when he pops back out, he is wearing his mystery solving hat and carrying his Personal Explorer Tablet—or P.E.T. for short.

The one with the Magnifying Glass App, the Camera App, the File App, and the Drawing App.

"Okay Boys, are we ready?" Jon Dart asks.
"Yep!" Zeus says.
"Yup!" Xerxes says.
Zeus, Xerxes, and Jon Dart return to the sandbox to...

INVESTIGATE!

Jon Dart presses the Magnifying Glass App on his PET and they all take a closer look at the footprints.

 Jon Dart taps the Drawing App on his PET and draws the footprints.

He then writes down some important things to remember about the footprints.

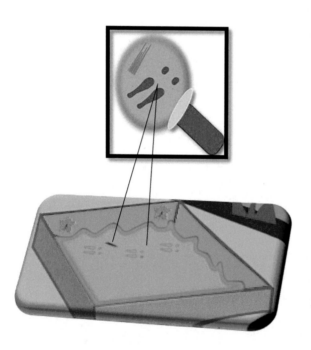

DART NOTES

➢ How many feet make up the footprints? Four feet

➢ Are they all the same? No—2 are the same and 2 are different

➢ Was there anything left near the footprints?

➢ Yes - a few blades of grass

"Let's look around and see where the footprints lead so we can begin our quest," Jon Dart says. Xerxes raises his nose to the sky and sniffs...

Zeus lowers his nose to the ground and sniffs...

Jon Dart looks around and says, "The footprints make up tracks that go this way, follow me Boys!"

Zeus, Xerxes and Jon Dart follow the tracks and meet Groundhog foraging in the grass. They introduce themselves and explain their quest.

"We are following tracks," Zeus says. "We need your help," Xerxes says.
"Can we look at your paws?" Jon Dart asks.
Groundhog nods his head and shows the trio his paws.

Jon Dart presses the Magnifying Glass App on the PET to first check his fore paws and then his hind paws.

DART NOTES

➤ Groundhogs are mammals

➤ Groundhogs have 4 toes on their fore paws and 5 toes on their hind paws

➤ Groundhogs live in underground burrows in wooded or bushy areas

➤ Groundhogs use a high pitched whistle to warn others when they sense danger

➤ Groundhogs are herbivores

Jon Dart taps the Writing App to check his notes. He also adds what they have learned about their new ground-hog friend.

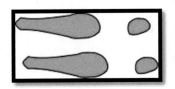

Jon Dart looks up at Zeus and scratches his head, "Sorry Boys—not a match," he says.

"Thanks for your help," Zeus says.

"You're welcome," Groundhog says and continues with his foraging.

"Have a good day," Xerxes says.

"Let's go Boys," Jon Dart says.

Zeus, Xerxes and Jon Dart continue to follow the tracks and meet Finch at the edge of the sunflower patch. They introduce themselves and explain their quest.

"We are following tracks," Zeus says.
"We need your help," Xerxes says.
"Can we look at your feet?" Jon Dart asks.
Finch flaps her wings and shows the trio her feet.

Jon Dart presses the Magnifying Glass App on the PET to first check her left foot and then her right foot.

Jon Dart taps the Writing App to check his notes. He also adds what they have learned about their new finch friend.

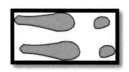

18

"Sorry Boys—not a match," Jon Dart says.

"Thanks for your help," Zeus says.

"You're welcome," Finch says and returns to the edge of the sunflower patch.

"See you around," Xerxes says.

"Off we go Boys," Jon Dart says.

The three friends continue on their way and follow the tracks one more time. They meet Rabbit at the entrance to her hole just under the azalea bushes. They introduce themselves and explain their quest again.

"We are following tracks," Zeus says. "We need your help," Xerxes says.

"Can we look at your paws?" Jon Dart asks.

Rabbit shakes her tail, then twitches her ears and shows the trio her paws.

Jon Dart presses the Magnifying Glass App on the PET to first check her fore paws and then her hind paws.

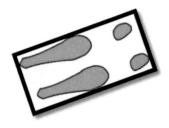

Dart Notes

➢ Rabbits are mammals

➢ Rabbits live in holes in the ground

➢ Rabbits have 5 toes on their fore paws and 4 toes on their hind paws

➢ Rabbits have long ears and bushy tails

➢ Rabbits are herbivores

Jon Dart taps the Writing App to check his notes. He also adds what they have learned about their new rabbit friend.

Jon Dart looks up and says, "We have a match Boys."

"Yes! Xerxes exclaims.

"We know the footprints don't belong to Groundhog," Jon Dart says.

"He only has four toes on his fore paws," Xerxes says.

"We know those footprints don't belong to Finch," Jon Dart says.

"She only has two feet," Zeus says.

"Those footprints you found in the sandbox belong to Rabbit," Jon Dart says.

Zeus and Xerxes jump around and shout…

"HOORAY!"

Well done Boys!

 *Jon Dart clicks the Camera App and takes a picture of the rabbit and then puts it next to the drawing of the paw prints they found in the sandbox.*

 *Lastly, Jon Dart opens the File App and adds the picture of the rabbit and the paw prints to the file.*

DART NOTES

Rabbit

Footprints

23

Once their quest is complete, Zeus, Xerxes, Jon Dart, and Rabbit celebrate and play together. Then...

Tatiana, Raquel, Zeus, Xerxes...time to come inside.

"Is that your mom?" Rabbit asks.

"No, that's our big sister, Jasmine," Zeus and Xerxes reply.

"I hear my mom calling me! Goodbye Zeus, goodbye Xerxes, goodbye Jon Dart," Rabbit says.

"Goodbye Rabbit, goodbye Boys, see you soon!" Jon Dart says.

"Goodbye Rabbit, goodbye Jon Dart," Zeus and Xerxes say.

Rabbit hops back to the azalea bush and Jon Dart returns to his home under the diving board.

Raquel slides down the slide and Tatiana jumps off of the rocking horse and they both run back towards the house.

After the others leave, Zeus and Xerxes run back to the house, but before they head inside...

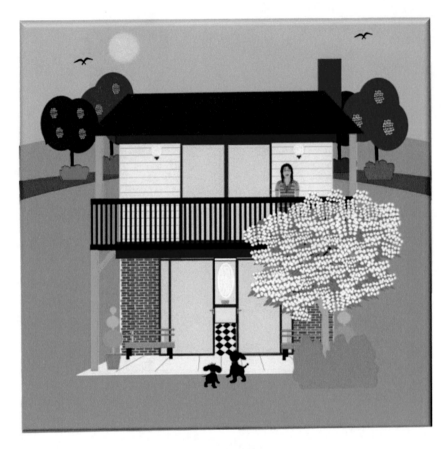

Zeus: Knock, knock.
Xerxes: Who's there?
Zeus: Etch.
Xerxes: Etch Who?
Zeus: God Bless you!
Xerxes: Little brother!

On their adventure Zeus, Xerxes, and Jon Dart met and learned about three animals that they found in their backyard – a groundhog, a finch and a rabbit. See who you find sharing your outdoor space when you look out your window and go out to play today.

GLOSSARY

BURROW – a hole in the ground made by an animal for shelter

FORE - front

FORAGING – looking around or searching for food

GRANIVORE – an animal that gets its energy from eating mainly seeds

HERBIVORE – an animal that gets its energy from eating plants

HIND - back

INVESTIGATE – to look closer

MAMMAL – a warm-blooded animal covered with hair or fur

QUEST – a search for something important

TRIO – a set or group of three things

XERXES (Zerk-cees) – the big brother

ZEUS (Zoose) – the little brother

25271413R00019

Made in the USA
Middletown, DE
24 October 2015